Cats

coloring book

THIS BOOK BELONGS TO

THANK YOU FOR CHOOSING OUR BOOK!

WITH THIS BOOK YOU WILL DISCOVER THE FASCINATING WORLD OF CATS. IT IS DESIGNED TO IMMERSE YOU IN A CREATIVE JOURNEY FILLED WITH FELINE CHARM AND RELAXATION.

WE REALLY WANT THIS COLORING BOOK TO FILL YOUR TIME WITH JOY AND RELAXATION. IF YOU LIKE IT, WE WOULD APPRECIATE A REVIEW ON AMAZON. YOUR REVIEW WILL NOT ONLY SUPPORT US, BUT ALSO HELP OTHERS FIND AND ENJOY OUR CREATION. ENJOY YOUR COLORING!

THANK YOU FOR CHOOSING OUR BOOK!

WITH THIS BOOK YOU WILL DISCOVER THE FASCINATING WORLD OF CATS. IT IS DESIGNED TO IMMERSE YOU IN A CREATIVE JOURNEY FILLED WITH SERENE CHARM AND RELAXATION.

WE REALLY WANT THIS COLORING BOOK TO FILL YOUR TIME WITH JOY AND RELAXATION IF YOU LIKE IT, WE WOULD APPRECIATE A REVIEW ON AMAZON. YOUR REVIEW WILL NOT ONLY SUPPORT US, BUT ALSO HELP OTHERS FIND AND ENJOY OUR CREATION.

ENJOY YOUR COLORING!

COLOR TEST PAGE

Made in the USA
Monee, IL
17 November 2024

70331838R00059